The Crazy Classroom Dictionary

By Rick Detorie

TOR

A TOM DOHERTY ASSOCIATES BOOK
NEW YORK

THE CRAZY CLASSROOM DICTIONARY

Copyright © 1993 by RGA Publishing Group, Inc.

Cover art by Rick Detorie
Interior art by Rick Detorie

A Tor Book
Published by Tom Doherty Associates, Inc.
175 Fifth Avenue
New York, N.Y. 10010

Tor® is a registered trademark of Tom Doherty Associates, Inc.

ISBN: 0-812-59432-0

First edition: September 1993

Printed in the United States of America

0 9 8 7 6 5 4 3 2 1

ap point' ment (doctor's, dentist's, etc.) n. a great reason to get out of class.

art n. a picture you slap together that looks pretty bad until your mom frames it and hangs it in the living room.

as sem´ bly n. a gathering at which the student body gets to see and be bored in person by the people they usually hear over the loudspeaker.

as sis´ tant prin´ ci pal n. the administrator in charge of discipline who always seems to know and remember everything about you.

bath´ room n. the place you go when you want to avoid answering a question.

caf´ e te´ ri a n. the place where they make good all-purpose cement, super glue, and colorful gravel.

ca reer´ day n. the day when adults come to class and describe their jobs. The most interesting careers involve props.

chalk´ board n. the thing the teacher faces to allow you to fool around.

class of´ fi cers n. pl. slick youngsters who spend all their allowance to win a campaign (most of them later run for the U.S. presidency).

class pic´ ture n. a group photo in which only the kids standing next to the teacher smile politely.

FOURTH GRADE
4-C
MRS. BOWERS

clock n. the thing on the wall that never seems to move.

com´ pass n. the thing that stabs you every time you reach into your pencil case.

com pu´ ter n. an electronic machine that students waste time on until the teacher's back is turned and they can play IAGO or STUNT COPTER or another computer game.

desk n. where most students sleep.

dra mat´ ics (school play) n. a performing event that often allows students to see and experience the four basic food groups complaining and getting sick.

drink´ ing foun´ tain n. the thing you have your face shoved into when someone in line pushes.

e ras´ ers n. pl. classroom weapons. Most effective when tossed at dark hair or dark clothing.

es´ say n. an exercise in writing and counting words, writing and counting words, writing and counting words...

fire drill n. an unexpected but welcome break from the classroom routine. Kind of like recess, except you have to fool around in line.

grades n. pl. like the weather, grades are something everyone talks about, but no one seems to do anything about.

grad u a´ tion n. the ceremony where parents stand around and cry about how old they're getting.

hall mon´ i tor n. the cave-dweller who checks hall passes.

hall pass n. what you sometimes need to go down the hall and into the bathroom.

hand n. the thing you raise in the classroom for attention. There are four varieties of hand-waving. 1, the "Me, me, me!" 2, the "Not really." 3, the prop. 4, the reverse headlock.

hob´ by day n. an in-class opportunity for students to display their personal hobbies. All of the hobbies are extremely boring, with the exception of a collection of live snakes.

home´ work n. something for which there are 6,874 reasons to forget to bring it to school.

home´ work proj´ ect n. the take-home project your parents offer to help you with, then end up doing entirely by themselves.

hy′ giene n. a class on health that teaches you things you learned in preschool.

in´ di vid´ u al pic´ ture n. a photo that shows the world how beautiful you are, and also how forgetful.

li´ brar´ y n. the only place where you can eat lunch in peace and quiet.

lock´ er n. a smaller version of a kid's room.

lunch n. what you eat at noon and almost until one o'clock when you're surprised with a pop quiz.

mu´ sic ap pre´ ci a´ tion n. a class during which you try not to laugh or crack your knuckles while listening to "serious" music.

notes n. pl. 1, what you pretend to take when the teacher is looking at you. 2, what you pass to friends when the teacher isn't looking at you.

nurse n. the person who, when you're not feeling well, calls your mother or father to make them feel guilty about it.

nu tri' tion n. a lesson during which the teacher tells you something you already know: food that's good for you always tastes bad.

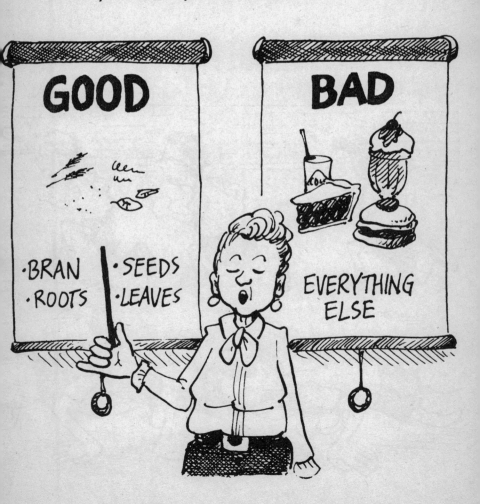

GOOD

BAD

·BRAN   ·SEEDS
·ROOTS ·LEAVES

EVERYTHING
ELSE

P.E. (Physical Education) n. approved, organized mass torture.

prin´ ci pal n. the school's head honcho. A person who sounds big and scary over the loudspeaker, but looks and sounds different in person.

qui´ et time n. a polite way for teachers to say "shut up."

rain´ y day ac tiv´ i ties n. pl.
crazy, desperate games that teachers
come up with when everyone has to
spend recess indoors.

re port´ card n. that thing you don't think about until it's too late.

sec´ re tar´ y n. the nice lady you try not to look at while you sit outside the assistant principal's office.

show 'n' tell n. a chance for students to display and brag about some of their weirder stuff.

spell´ ing bee n. a competition that makes you a nervous wreck until you miss a word and can sit and enjoy watching the other kids mess up.

teach´ er n. the grown-up at the front of the classroom who has a collection of mugs, trophies, and plaques gathering dust in the closet at home.